An Egg Is An Egg

written and illustrated by

NICKI WEISS

G. P. Putnam's Sons New York

Text and illustrations copyright © 1990 by Monica J. Weiss
All rights reserved. This book, or parts thereof, may not be reproduced
in any form without permission in writing from the publisher.
G.P. Putnam's Sons, a division of The Putnam & Grosset Group,
200 Madison Avenue, New York, NY 10016
Published simultaneously in Canada.
Printed in Hong Kong by South China Printing Co. (1988) Ltd.
Book design by Golda Laurens

Library of Congress Cataloging-in-Publication Data
Weiss, Nicki. An egg is an egg / Nicki Weiss. p. cm.
Summary: A poetic explanation of how everything changes—eggs
to chicks, branches to sticks, green to white, and day to night.
[1. Change—Fiction. 2. Stories in rhyme.] I. Title.
PZ8.3.W425Eg 1990 [E]—dc20 89-8462 CIP AC
ISBN 0-399-22182-4
1 3 5 7 9 10 8 6 4 2
First impression

For Rachel

An egg is an egg
Until it hatches.

And then it is a chick.

A branch is a branch
Until it breaks.

And then it is a stick.

Nothing stays the same.
Everything can change.

A seed is a seed
Until it is sown.

And then it is a flower.

A block is a block
Until there are many.

And then they become a tower.

Nothing stays the same.
Everything can change.

Water is water
Until it is brewed.

And then it becomes tea.

You are you
Until I come.

And then you become "we."

Nothing stays the same.
Everything can change.

The yard is green
Until it snows.

And then it becomes white.

Day is day
Until sunset.

And then it is the night.

Nothing stays the same.
Everything can change.

This baby was a baby
Until he grew.

And now he is a boy.

But you can always be a baby.

You will always be my baby.....

Some things stay the same.
Some things never change.